Dot.™

For Pet's Sake

Dot.™
For Pet's Sake

**CANDLEWICK
ENTERTAINMENT**

Jim Henson™
THE JIM HENSON COMPANY

First edition 2020

Library of Congress Catalog Card Number pending
ISBN 978-1-5362-1656-1

20 21 22 23 24 25 CCP 10 9 8 7 6 5 4 3 2 1

Printed in Shenzhen, Guangdong, China

This book was typeset in Brandon Grotesque Bold.
The illustrations were created digitally.

Candlewick Entertainment
an imprint of
Candlewick Press
99 Dover Street
Somerville, Massachusetts 02144

www.candlewick.com

Contents

Chapter 1

· · · · · · · ·

Dot's kitchen was full of people. And pets.

"It's really nice of you to look after my cat, Meryl, while we're gone this weekend, Dot," said Dot's friend Ruby.

"We'll have tons of fun," said Dot. "Meryl, Scratch, and I will be like the three musketeers!"

"Here are her things," Ruby's mom said, holding a bag of supplies. "Thank you so much."

"You're very welcome," said Dot's mom. "It will be a great experience for Dot *and* Meryl."

"Yup!" said Dot. "I even got this new Pet Pal app so I can take care of all of Meryl's needs easily."

Dot took out her tablet and opened up the Pet Pal app. "So, what do I need to know?"

"Make sure her water dish is always full," said Ruby.

"And give her dry food twice a day and wet food once a day. And treats when she's a good kitty!"

Dot tapped the food and water icons on her app.

"And scoop her litter box after she goes to the bathroom."

"Litter box?" said Dot.

"Meryl is an *indoor* cat, so she does all her business inside," said Ruby's mom, handing Dot a litter scoop.

"Got it," said Dot, adding a note to the Pet Pal app.

"And whatever you do," said Ruby, "DON'T let her outside!"

"Right. Business inside, no going outside. No problem!" said Dot.

Ruby and her mom headed for the door.

"Bye, Meryl! I'll miss you," said Ruby. "Thanks, Dot!"

Chapter 2

· · · · · · · · ·

"**Y**ou two are going to be best friends, I know it," Dot said to Meryl and Scratch. Meryl hissed. ". . . Just as soon as Meryl gets comfortable here!"

The Pet Pal app dinged. It was time to fill Meryl's water and food bowls. Dot got out the bag of cat food just as there was a knock at the back door. Dot's friend Hal was there, dressed up like a veterinarian.

"Hi, Dot. Your pet assistant, Dr. Hal, has arrived." Hal was holding a bowl with a goldfish in it. He slid the door open.

"Hal, don't let the cat out!" Dot cried as Meryl bolted for the open door.

"Huh?" said Hal. "Oh!"

He closed the
door just in time.

Hal held up the fish bowl. "I thought Sir Gilderson would like some company. He doesn't get out much."

Dot giggled.

"Well, if we're going to take care of two pets, we might as well take care of three." She opened her Pet Pal app. "What do we need to do for Sir Gilderson?"

"Just feed him twice a day," said Hal.

"Easy peasy!" said Dot.

The doorbell rang.

Chapter 3

· · · · · · · ·

Two more of Dot's friends were at the door. One had a birdcage. The other held a glass terrarium.

"Hi, Nev. Hi, Dev," said Dot, smiling at the twins.

"We heard about your pet-sitting service!" said Nev.

"Wow, word travels fast," said Hal.

"We thought maybe you could look after our pets while we clean all the pudding out of our room," said Dev.

Dot and Hal looked perplexed.

"Don't ask," said Dev.

"So, will you look after

Zippington and Waldo?" asked Nev.

Dev held up the terrarium.

"Is that a . . . *spider*?" gasped Hal.

He hated spiders.

"No, silly, Waldo is a tarantula," said Dev.

"Don't worry, he doesn't bite," said Nev. "Unless he gets scared."

Hal backed away from the terrarium.

"Hmm. We already have Scratch,
Meryl, *and* Sir Gilderson," said
Dot. "But if we can look after three
pets, we may as well look after five!
Besides, my Pet Pal app will make it
a breeze."

Chapter 4

. . . .

Dot carried Zippington's birdcage into the living room. Hal brought in Waldo's terrarium, holding it at arm's length.

"Relax, Hal," said Dot. "Dev says Waldo is more afraid of you than you are of him."

"Then he must be *pretty* afraid," said Hal.

Suddenly Meryl and Scratch came dashing into the room, barking and hissing at each other.

"Whoa!" yelled Hal as they ran by, narrowly missing the terrarium.

"Scratch! Meryl! Stop it!" shouted Dot. She put the birdcage down.

"I'll get Scratch," she said, running after the dog. "You grab Meryl."

"Anything to get out of spider duty," Hal said, putting the terrarium on the table.

Meryl leaped up onto the armchair.

"Good kitty," Hal said, reaching out his arms. "Ahh!"

Meryl jumped straight over Hal

and onto the table, knocking the

lid off Waldo's terrarium before

running out of the room.

"Come here, Meryl!" Hal called,

dashing after her.

No one noticed the tarantula had crawled out of his cage . . .

Chapter 5

· · · · · · · · ·

Dot finally got hold of Scratch as the Pet Pal app dinged.

"Feeding time for Sir Gilderson," Dot read off her tablet.

"I've got this one," Hal said, shaking fish food into Sir Gilderson's bowl. "Who's hungry?"

Meryl purred and jumped off the bookcase and onto the table, then swiped at the fish bowl.

"Meryl!" Hal said. "It's *fish* feeding time, not *cat* feeding time!"

Scratch barked.

Dot picked up Meryl and walked
over to the bag Ruby's mom had left.
"We need something to keep Meryl
busy, just until all the pets get used to
one another." She fished out a
toy mouse. "Perfect!"

Dot set the toy on the ground and Meryl chased it happily around the room.

"That's it, girl!" Dot picked up another toy. "And Scratch, here's Mr.

Socky for you! There's a good boy!"

Scratch grabbed the toy in his mouth and squeezed it.

"Pet sitting is harder than I thought!" Dot said. "But I've got the hang of it now."

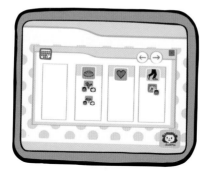

Chapter 6

· · · · · · · · ·

Dot checked her tablet. "Okay, the Pet Pal app says it's time to feed Zippington and Waldo *and* take Scratch for a walk."

"That's a lot," said Hal.

"We can do it," said Dot. "First

we'll feed Zippington and Waldo, then you can take Scratch for a walk while I look after the other pets."

"What do we feed Zippington again?" asked Hal.

Dot checked the app and handed Hal a small box.

Hal opened it up. It was full of crickets.

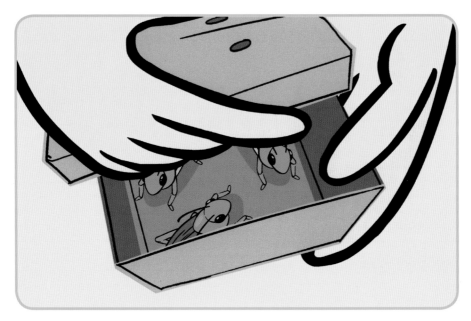

"The app says to give her one of these," Dot said.

Hal opened up the door of the birdcage, putting a cricket inside.

Zippington squawked. She did not look happy.

Dot looked at her app again. "Oh, no!" She held up a box of birdseed. "Sorry, Zippington! That was Waldo's food."

Hal reached into the cage to take out the cricket, and Zippington flew straight out.

"Oh, *no*," Dot groaned.

Scratch barked at the flying bird.
"Sit, Scratch," said Dot. "Don't scare
her."

"Here," said Hal, handing the
cricket to Dot. "You feed Waldo
while I catch the bird."

"Ick," said Dot, walking over
to the terrarium and dropping the
cricket inside. She got closer
and peered into it. "Um, Hal?" Dot
got down on her hands and knees

and looked under the table. "We *may* have a tarantula on the loose . . ."

"Ahh!" Hal yelled, jumping onto the couch.

Chapter 7

. . . .

Dot surveyed the room. "Okay, I've been a pet sitter for about twenty minutes. I can totally handle this." She looked under the armchair and made a face. "I think *maybe* we have too many pets."

"As a pretend vet, I agree," Hal said as he tried to catch Zippington.

"Waldo must be *somewhere*!" Dot cried as the bird swooped around the room and Scratch barked. "I know, Scratch, it's time for your walk."

She led the dog over to the door. "Why don't you wait in the backyard?" Scratch ran outside and Dot pushed the sliding door shut, but it bounced back open a crack.

"Waldo? Waldo!" she called, walking around the room. Then her tablet started dinging.

"Dot, the Pet Pal app!" said Hal.

"I know," cried Dot, "but we have to find Waldo!"

Then Meryl started yowling. There was a tarantula in her water bowl!

"There's Waldo!" yelled Dot and Hal in relief.

Meryl hissed and leaped away from the tarantula—right toward the open door!

"And there goes Meryl!" Dot yelled, running after the cat into the backyard.

Meryl jumped onto the fence at the edge of the yard.

"Meryl! Come down now!"

Dot cried.

Meryl took one look at Dot—
and jumped straight over the fence.

Chapter 8

· · · · · · · ·

Dot and her mom walked through the neighborhood, Scratch trotting along beside them. Dot shook a bag of cat treats. "Here, Meryl! Come here, girl!" she called.

"Sorry, Mom," she said.

"Well, you did bite off a little more than you could chew, honey," said Mom. "But I'm glad you asked for help."

"I thought I could take care of all these pets," Dot said. "But I had so many, I wasn't taking care of *any* of them very well."

Suddenly Scratch began barking.
Meryl was right across the street!
She was on the porch of Ruby's
house, pawing at the door.

Mom and Dot broke into a run.
"Meryl! There you are!" called Dot.
"Poor kitty—you must miss Ruby. I
know I do!"

Dot rubbed Meryl's cheeks.
"Sorry I didn't take very good care of
you. But I promise to give you all the
attention you need now." She looked
at Mom. "Maybe we should take the
other pets home?"

"Sounds like a plan," agreed Mom.
"Speaking of the other pets, I wonder
how your dad and Hal are doing . . ."

Chapter 9

· · · · · · · · ·

Dot's dad carefully placed Zippington back into her birdcage. Hal approached him from behind, carrying the glass terrarium.

"Thanks for getting Zippington, Mr. C. I couldn't have done it without you," Hal said.

"No problem, Hal," said Dad.

"Also," said Hal, "I wouldn't sit down if I were you . . ." The tarantula was crawling right up Dad's back!

Hal lifted the terrarium and took a deep breath. He carefully scooped Waldo up and back into it, then quickly put the lid back on.

"Oh!" said Dad. "Nice catch!"

Hal shuddered. He looked into Waldo's terrarium. "I guess you're not so bad," he said to the tarantula. Waldo stood up on his hind legs and waved at Hal. "Ahh!" Hal yelped.

"**O**nce I focused on taking care of Meryl and Scratch—and *only* Meryl and Scratch—things got a lot better. Plus, they turned out to be pretty good buddies!

"Oh! I think Ruby's here to get Meryl. Time for my *paw*-sitively *purr*fect guest to go back home.

"And that means it's time for me to unplug. This is Dot, signing off for now!"